Associated Board Brass Scales and Arpeggios

Series Editors **John Wallace** and **Ian Denley**

Scales and Arpeggios for Trumpet and Brass Band instruments 𝄞

Grades 1-8

Trumpet, Cornet, Flugelhorn, E♭ Horn, Baritone 𝄞 Euphonium 𝄞, Trombone 𝄞, Tuba 𝄞

It is often maintained, with some justification, that brass-players frequently show reluctance to learn scales and arpeggios thoroughly. But as they form the basis of a fluent technique, a methodical and thorough preparation of scales and arpeggios is essential: they stabilize range and accuracy and provide the foundation on which further skills such as transposition can be built.

This manual seeks to assist this situation by including comprehensive fingering and trombone slide position charts, together with hints on problems to avoid and useful advice appended to the scales and arpeggios most likely to be problematic. The aim is to help students learn their scales and arpeggios thoroughly, as well as provide support material for those brass teachers who may not be specialists on this group of instruments.

Given the wide range of instruments catered for in this manual, we are most grateful to the following team of contributing specialist advisers: Ray Allen, Senior Professor of Trumpet at the Royal Academy of Music; Richard Grantham, Director of Music at the Headlands School, Bridlington; Dudley Bright, Principal Trombone with the Philharmonia Orchestra and Professor at the Royal Academy of Music; Peter Walker, a member of the brass teaching team of the North Yorkshire Education Authority; Bob Childs, Head of Brass at Hymers College, Hull, and Principal Euphonium of the Black Dyke Mills Brass Band; and Patrick Harrild, Principal Tuba with the London Symphony Orchestra and Professor at the Royal Academy of Music and the Guildhall School of Music.

JOHN WALLACE and IAN DENLEY   1995

The Associated Board of the Royal Schools of Music

Valved instrument fingering chart

This comprehensive fingering chart applies to the trumpet and those valved brass instruments which read in the treble clef. Both standard and alternative fingerings available to the trumpet, cornet (B♭ and E♭ soprano), flugelhorn, E♭ horn (tenor horn), baritone, euphonium and tuba are given. Additional information is given in the annotations attached to the scales and arpeggios.

The first six fingerings (C–F), which are for notes below the range required in the Associated Board's examinations, are included for their presence in some repertoire. The shaded fingerings are available only to euphoniums and tubas which have a 4th valve (see note on the 4th valve on p.5).

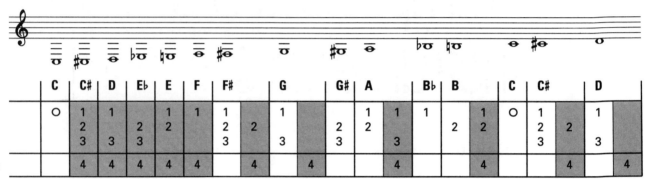

	C	C#	D	E♭	E	F	F#	G	G#	A	B♭	B	C	C#	D
Fingering	O	1 2 3	1 3	2 3	1 2 3	1 2	1 2 3	1 · 2 3	2 3	1 2 · 1 3	1	2 · 1 2	O	1 2 3	2 · 1 3
4th valve		4	4	4	4		4		4	4		4		4	4

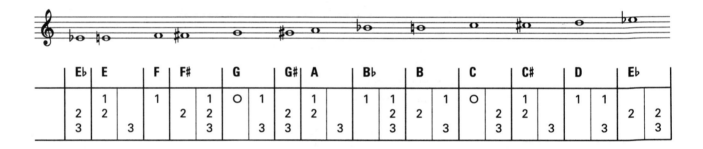

	E♭	E	F	F#	G	G#	A	B♭	B	C	C#	D	E♭
Fingering	2 3	1 2 · 3	1	2 · 1 2 3	O · 1 3	2 3	1 2 · 3	1 · 1 2 3	2 · 3	O · 2 3	1 2 · 3	1 · 3	2 · 2 3

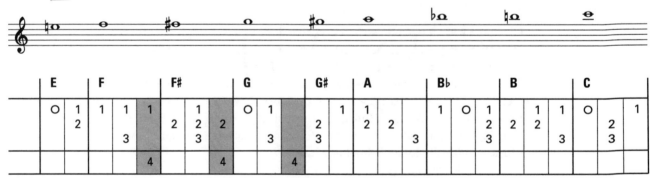

	E	F	F#	G	G#	A	B♭	B	C
Fingering	O · 1 2	1 · 1 3	1 · 2 · 1 2 3	2 · O · 1 3	2 3 · 1	1 2 · 2 · 3	1 · O · 1 2 3	2 · 1 2 · 1 3	O · 2 3 · 1
4th valve			4	4		4			

Key to symbols

1	press index finger	3	press ring finger	4	press 4th valve (euphonium and tuba only).
2	press middle finger	O	all fingers off		Usually played by the LH middle finger.

© 1995 by The Associated Board of the Royal Schools of Music

Trombone slide position chart

This comprehensive slide position chart applies to the trombone when it is read in the treble clef. It gives the standard slide positions, together with alternatives available from the 'F' thumb valve (known also as the 'plug' or 'trigger') and indicates slide length adjustments which may be necessary in the upper register (see p.7 for details of these measurements).

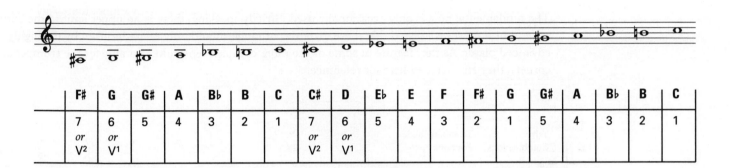

	F#	G	G#	A	B♭	B	C	C#	D	E♭	E	F	F#	G	G#	A	B♭	B	C
	7	6	5	4	3	2	1	7	6	5	4	3	2	1	5	4	3	2	1
	or	or						or	or										
	V²	V¹						V²	V¹										

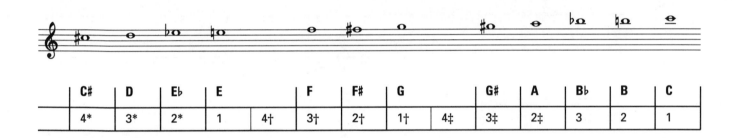

	C#	D	E♭	E		F	F#	G		G#	A	B♭	B	C
	4*	3*	2*	1	4†	3†	2†	1†	4‡	3‡	2‡	3	2	1

Key to symbols

1-7	basic slide positions
V¹	1st position + 'F' thumb valve (see p.7).
V²	2nd position + 'F' thumb valve (see p.7).

*⎫
†⎬ These symbols indicate the various slide
‡⎭ adjustments necessary to improve tuning.
See note on intonation on p.7.

Table of harmonics

As a source for the exploration of alternative fingerings, the following table illustrates the notes available from each combination of valves (i.e. each length of tubing). This is known as the *harmonic series*. The first note in each row is the 'fundamental' or 'pedal note'. The numbered notes which follow the fundamental, obtainable from each valve combination by embouchure adjustment, are known as *harmonics*, or *upper partials*.

The fundamental note is only occasionally used. Strictly speaking, there is no upper limit to the harmonic series, but it must be stressed that these extremes of range should only be undertaken by the highly advanced player. As they feature in some of the more complex repertoire (notably for the trumpet and cornet), they are included here for reference.

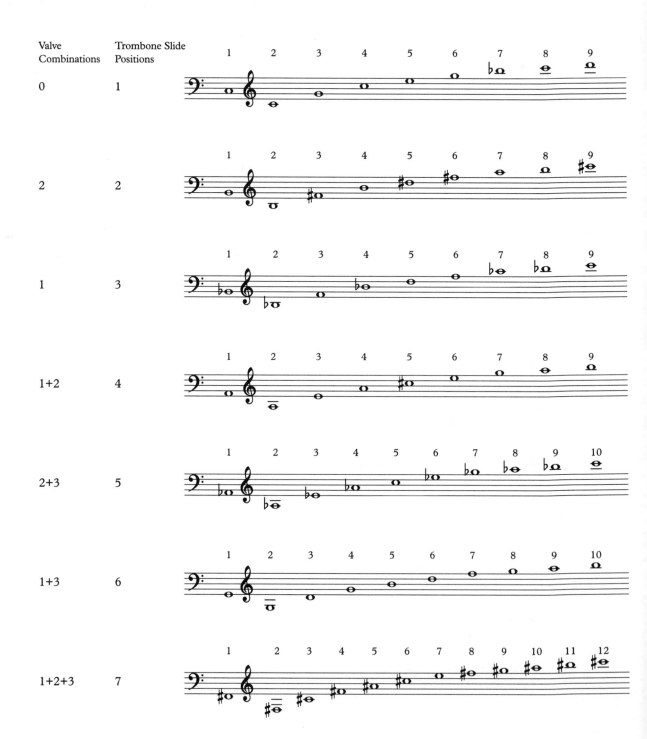

Guide to valved instruments

For reference purposes, where notes are indicated throughout the manual with a small superscript number (e.g. Bb^1, E^2, $F\#^3$, etc.), this refers to their position within the range of this family of brass instruments:

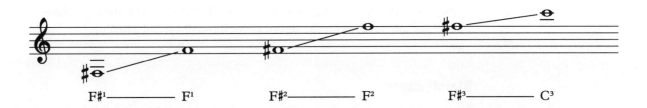

F#¹ ———— F¹   F#² ———— F²   F#³ ———— C³

The range of notes within the Associated Board's scales and arpeggios is from $F\#^1$ to C^3 ($F\#^1$ to Bb^3 for the Eb soprano cornet).

Posture, fingering and grip

The importance of developing a good posture (frequently overlooked by brass players) is essential in the process of natural breathing, which is vital in the study of scales and arpeggios. The parts of the body involved must be kept comfortably in balance, whether standing or sitting.

For really fluent scales and arpeggios the hand depressing the valves must be relaxed. Most of the weight bearing of the instrument should be taken by the other hand.

On the trumpet, cornet and flugelhorn the RH thumb should touch the underside of the 'lead-in' pipe to steady the hand, simultaneously allowing a balanced RH position with the hand at 90° to the instrument (on some older models of cornet care should be taken to avoid the RH thumb catching the 1st valve slide trigger where present). It is preferable that the little finger ring be used but only if it is comfortable and does not produce tension. A sideways pressure when depressing a valve should be avoided as it will impair the valve action.

The 4th valve (euphonium and tuba only)

The 4th valve is the most common additional valve found on the euphonium and tuba. It provides an excellent opportunity for options in tuning, as well as facility in fingering, and if available should always be used.

The Eb soprano cornet

In this instrument's lower register especially, intonation is not as stable as on the trumpet, Bb cornet or flugelhorn. Students should therefore listen to intonation extremely critically and should be encouraged to experiment with fingering alternatives where appropriate. In striving for a full, open sound across the range of the instrument, the importance of correct breathing and diaphragm support cannot be over-emphasized.

Intonation

Intonation and the careful negotiation of intervals should feature greatly in the study of scales and arpeggios. They are affected by many factors: the size of the oral cavity, the position of the tongue and the quality of the sound (quality of sound profoundly affects pitch).

Generally, the best fingering to use is the one that is in tune. This is especially true at the top of the range where the harmonics are closer together.

F#^{1}, C#^{1} and D^1 (below the treble stave), fingered 1+2+3, 1+2+3, and 1+3 respectively, are usually sharp on valved instruments. Most modern trumpets, cornets and flugelhorns have triggered or push/pull 1st and 3rd valve slides which can be extended a little to improve the intonation of these notes. Using the finger ring provided for this purpose may feel awkward at first, but with appropriate guidance, experience will eventually make this quite a normal manœuvre. Players of the euphonium and tuba can compensate by using the alternative fingerings involving the 4th valve where this is available.

On the euphonium and baritone top F, F# and G are also usually sharp. Euphonium players should compensate by using the 4th valve where available.

Players whose instruments do not possess either the 1st and 3rd valve slides or a 4th valve can learn to temper the intonation with the embouchure through careful listening.

Maintenance

It is important that all valves and tuning slides be kept lubricated for optimum performance.

Enharmonic note-names

Two or three notes having the same sound but different names are called *enharmonics*; for example, E♭ is the enharmonic of D♯. A full table is given below to guide students in the fingering of those notes in certain scales and arpeggios which may be unfamiliarly notated.

C	=	B♯	=	D♭♭		E	=	F♭	=	D𝄪		G♯	=	A♭		
C♯	=	D♭	=	B𝄪		F	=	E♯	=	G♭♭		A	=	G𝄪	=	B♭♭
D	=	C𝄪	=	E♭♭		F♯	=	G♭	=	E𝄪		B♭	=	A♯	=	C♭♭
E♭	=	D♯	=	F♭♭		G	=	F𝄪	=	A♭♭		B	=	C♭	=	A𝄪

Guide to trombone slide positions

For reference purposes, where notes are indicated throughout the manual with a small superscript number (e.g. B♭^{1}, E^2, F♯^{3}, etc.), this refers to their position within the trombone's range:

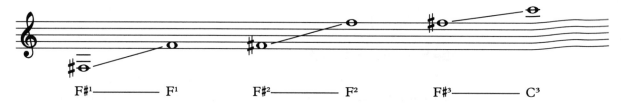

The range of notes within the Associated Board's scales and arpeggios is from F♯^{1} to C^3.

Slide positions

There are very few alternative positions which are used in scales and arpeggios. Those given for some notes in the upper register may be tried, but should be discarded if found to be unsatisfactory.

In reality, it is virtually impossible to measure the slide positions accurately, but it is important to be aware of their relative location and to understand that each position extends slightly further than the last. This will help avoid the common occurrence among inexperienced players of playing progressively sharper as the slide is extended further.

The following diagram illustrates the approximate measurement in centimetres of each slide position, as measured from the 1st or closed position:

position	1	2	3	4	5	6	7
cm.	0	8	16.5	26.5	37	48	60

'F' valve alternatives

Where available, the 'F' valve is used to avoid the long stretch of the 6th and 7th positions:

'F' valve + 1st position (V¹) = 6th position   'F' valve + 2nd position (V²) = 7th position

NB: when using the 'F' valve with 2nd position (V²), the slide should be extended to a length of 10 cm., not 8.

Intonation

The trombonist must learn to master intonation in the seven standard positions through careful listening, both to himself (or herself) and others with whom he (she) might be playing.

Due to the nature of its slide mechanism, perfect intonation on the trombone is more immediately accessible than on valved brass instruments. Whilst not every note in each position is exactly in tune, the slide can be used to make slight adjustments.

The slide position chart indicates, with the symbols *, † and ‡, those notes which may require adjustments to improve the tuning. In the measurements below, *minus* quantities indicate that the slide should be drawn *towards* the player by the suggested amount; *plus* quantities indicate that the slide should be extended *away* from the player.

* = −2-5mm.   † = +5-10mm.   ‡ = −15-20mm.

These are given only as a guide, as intonation varies between instruments. The importance of careful listening cannot be stressed enough in determining the extent of these small but significant adjustments.

Care should be taken to ensure that all notes are centred at their true pitch before slide adjustments are made. This skill is developed by a constant and discriminating attention to both tone quality and intonation.

Maintenance

It is important that the main slide and tuning slides be kept lubricated for optimum performance.

Enharmonic note-names

Two or three notes having the same sound but different names are called *enharmonics*; for example, E♭ is the enharmonic of D♯. A full table is given below to guide students in the fingering of those notes in certain scales and arpeggios which may be unfamiliarly notated.

C	=	B♯	=	D♭♭		E	=	F♭	=	D𝄪		G♯	=	A♭		
C♯	=	D♭	=	B𝄪		F	=	E♯	=	G♭♭		A	=	G𝄪	=	B♭♭
D	=	C𝄪	=	E♭♭		F♯	=	G♭	=	E𝄪		B♭	=	A♯	=	C♭♭
E♭	=	D♯	=	F♭♭		G	=	F𝄪	=	A♭♭		B	=	C♭	=	A𝄪

Notes on the requirements

Reference must always be made to the syllabus for the year in which the examination is to be taken, in case any changes have been made to the requirements.

In the examination all scales and arpeggios must be played from memory.

Candidates should aim to play their scales and arpeggios at a pace that allows accuracy, with a uniform tone across all registers and a rhythmic flow without undue accentuation, as well as with even tonguing and good intonation. Recommended speeds for all instruments are given on page 11.

In Grades 1-5 candidates may choose *either* the melodic *or* the harmonic form of the minor scale; in Grades 6-8 candidates are required to play *both* forms.

The choice of breathing place is left to the candidate's discretion, but taking a breath must not be allowed to disturb the flow of the scale or arpeggio. In the case of valved instruments, if a breath is taken during the course of a slurred scale or arpeggio, a *soft* tongue attack should be made on the note following the breath.

It is desirable that students do not use a breath as a means of disguising an embouchure 'break', where the position of the lips on the mouthpiece has to be re-seated as the player moves from one register to another in the course of a scale or arpeggio. Whilst embouchure breaks are quite common, it is preferable to be free from them as they do cause difficulties and can be avoided. Given the enormous amount of breath required by the tuba, especially in its lowest range, students should aim for the best musical result by keeping the unavoidably frequent breaths as unostentatious as possible.

Articulation

It is very important for the foundation of good articulation that players use the *tongue* to articulate, rather than just the breath, which is a common error at the elementary level. The sound must be well-supported by diaphragmatic breathing throughout all forms of articulation, so that the tone does not deteriorate (usually with attendant intonation problems), especially when tonguing *staccato*.

Four different forms of articulation are found in the scale and arpeggio requirements: slurred, tongued, *legato*-tongued and *staccato*.

Valved instruments	In Grades 1-6 candidates are required to play scales and arpeggios both slurred and tongued; in Grades 7 and 8 candidates are required to play scales and arpeggios slurred, *legato*-tongued and *staccato*.
Trombone	In Grades 1-6 candidates are required to play scales and arpeggios both tongued and *legato*-tongued; in Grades 7 and 8 candidates are required to play scales and arpeggios tongued, *legato*-tongued and *staccato*.

In slurred scales and arpeggios there is no gap between the notes, whereas the gap is large when playing *staccato*. In *legato*-tonguing the effect is almost slurred, but there is the smallest separation achieved by a very soft tongue attack.

The articulations may be visualized like this:

slurred   _____

tongued   ____   ____   ____   ____

legato-tongued _____ _____ _____ _____

staccato   __   __   __   __

Legato-tonguing is often considered by brass players to be a fusion of *tenuto* and *legato*; it is sometimes described as 'soft'-tonguing or as an articulated slur. Perhaps the least familiar of the articulation forms required, it may usefully be notated as follows:

Considerations for the trombonist

It is especially important that trombonists make a clear distinction between tongued and *legato*-tongued in all grades. Trombonists do not have the option of slurring in the accepted sense of the word and must develop a really smooth and accurate slide-control from the earliest stages to expect real success in achieving *legato* effects on their instrument. This is best achieved by moving the slide as quickly as possible, without gripping or jerking it. The major difficulty lies in avoiding smears or *glissando*s when the slide has to move in the same direction as the pitch.

A 'soft' consonant should be used to tongue as the slide is moved. It should be soft enough to keep the *legato* smooth without interrupting the sound, but firm enough to avoid making a *glissando*.

A relaxed posture and open throat will help keep the breath flow even and continuous, thereby avoiding bulges and unscheduled accents in what should be essentially smooth lines.

Current requirements for Grades 1-8

These tables list scales and arpeggios required for each grade; numbers refer to those printed alongside the scales and arpeggios in the following pages.

Trumpet, B♭ Cornet, Flugelhorn, E♭ Horn (Tenor Horn), Baritone, Euphonium, Tuba

Grade 1   1, 54 *or* 55, 84, 122

Grade 2   5, 19, 32 *or* 33, 54 *or* 55, 88, 102, 111, 122

Grade 3   7, 9, 17, 24 *or* 25, 38 *or* 39, 68, 90, 92, 100, 107, 114

Grade 4   11, 15, 20, 4   43,   57,   65, 77, 94, 98, 103, 116, 123, 127

Grade 5   4, 14, 16, 20,   31,   51,   61, 69, 87, 97, 99, 103, 110, 120, 125, 129

Grade 6   6, 13, 18, 21, 26, 27, 52, 53, 58, 59, 62, 63, 73, 74, 75, 76, 89, 96, 101, 104, 108, 121, 124, 126, 131, 136

Grade 7   2, 4, 6, 8, 10, 12, 13, 14, 16, 18, 21, 23, 26, 27, 30, 31, 34, 35, 36, 37, 40, 41, 44, 45, 48, 49, 50, 51, 52, 53, 58, 59, 62, 63, 66, 67, 73, 74, 75, 76, 78, 79, 85, 87, 89, 91, 93, 95, 96, 97, 99, 101, 104, 106, 108, 110, 112, 113, 115, 117, 119, 120, 121, 124, 126, 128, 129, 130, 132, 137, 138

Grade 8   3, 4, 6, 8, 10, 12, 13, 14, 16, 18, 21, 23, 28, 29, 30, 31, 34, 35, 36, 37, 40, 41, 44, 45, 48, 49, 50, 51, 52, 53, 58, 59, 62, 63, 66, 67, 70, 73, 74, 75, 76, 78, 79, 82, 83, 86, 87, 89, 91, 93, 95, 96, 97, 99, 101, 104, 106, 109, 110, 112, 113, 115, 117, 119, 120, 121, 124, 126, 128, 129, 130, 131, 132, 133, 134, 135, 137, 138, 139

E♭ Soprano Cornet

Grade 1   1, 54 *or* 55, 84, 122

Grade 2   5, 19, 32 *or* 33, 54 *or* 55, 88, 102, 111, 122

Grade 3   7, 9, 17, 24 *or* 25, 38 *or* 39, 68, 90, 92, 100, 107, 114

Grade 4   11, 15, 20, 42 *or* 43, 56 *or* 57, 64 *or* 65, 77, 94, 98, 103, 116, 123, 127

Grade 5   4, 14, 16, 20, 30 *or* 31, 50 *or* 51, 60 *or* 61, 69, 87, 97, 99, 103, 110, 120, 125, 129

Grade 6   6, 13, 18, 20, 26, 27, 52, 53, 58, 59, 60, 61, 73, 74, 75, 76, 89, 96, 101, 103, 108, 121, 124, 125, 131, 136

Grade 7   2, 4, 6, 13, 14, 16, 18, 20, 22, 26, 27, 30, 31, 34, 35, 48, 49, 50, 51, 52, 53, 58, 59, 60, 61, 64, 65, 73, 74, 75, 76, 85, 87, 89, 96, 97, 99, 101, 103, 105, 108, 110, 112, 119, 120, 121, 124, 125, 127, 129, 130, 137, 138

Grade 8   2, 4, 6, 8, 13, 14, 16, 18, 21, 22, 26, 27, 30, 31, 34, 35, 36, 37, 48, 49, 50, 51, 52, 53, 58, 59, 62, 63, 64, 65, 73, 74, 75, 76, 78, 80, 81, 85, 87, 89, 91, 96, 97, 99, 101, 104, 105, 108, 110, 112, 113, 119, 120, 121, 124, 126, 129, 130, 131, 132, 135, 137, 138, 139

Trombone

Grade 1   1, 32 *or* 33, 84, 111

Grade 2   5, 19, 32 *or* 33, 38 *or* 39, 88, 102, 111, 114

Grade 3   9, 11, 20, 38 *or* 39, 56 *or* 57, 71, 92, 94, 103, 114, 123

Grade 4   2, 7, 20, 46 *or* 47, 56 *or* 57, 72, 85, 90, 103, 118, 123

Grade 5   14, 16, 18, 22, 34 *or* 35, 50 *or* 51, 58 *or* 59, 74, 97, 99, 101, 105, 112, 120, 124, 129

Grade 6   2, 6, 13, 21, 26, 27, 36, 37, 52, 53, 76, 78, 85, 89, 96, 104, 108, 113, 121, 131, 136

Grade 7   3, 4, 6, 8, 10, 12, 13, 14, 16, 18, 21, 23, 28, 29, 30, 31, 34, 35, 36, 37, 40, 41, 44, 45, 48, 49, 50, 51, 52, 53, 58, 59, 62, 63, 66, 67, 70, 73, 74, 75, 76, 78, 79, 86, 87, 89, 91, 93, 95, 96, 97, 99, 101, 104, 106, 109, 110, 112, 113, 115, 117, 119, 120, 121, 124, 126, 128, 130, 132, 138, 140

Grade 8   3, 4, 6, 8, 10, 12, 13, 14, 16, 18, 21, 23, 28, 29, 30, 31, 34, 35, 36, 37, 40, 41, 44, 45, 48, 49, 50, 51, 52, 53, 58, 59, 62, 63, 66, 67, 70, 73, 74, 75, 76, 78, 79, 82, 83, 86, 87, 89, 91, 93, 95, 96, 97, 99, 101, 104, 106, 109, 110, 112, 113, 115, 117, 119, 120, 121, 124, 126, 128, 129, 130, 131, 132, 133, 134, 135, 138, 139, 140

Recommended speeds

The following recommended *minimum* speeds are given as a general guide. It is essential that scales and arpeggios are played at a speed rapid enough to allow well-organized breathing, yet steady enough to allow a well-focused sound with good intonation across the range.

Valved instruments

major and minor scales, chromatic scales, whole-tone scales, dominant and diminished sevenths				*major and minor arpeggios*		
Grade 1	♩	=	50	♪	=	72
Grade 2	♩	=	56	♪	=	80
Grade 3	♩	=	66	♪	=	92
Grade 4	♩	=	72	♪	=	100
Grade 5	♩	=	80	♪	=	112
Grade 6	♩	=	104	♩.	=	56
Grade 7	♩	=	116	♩.	=	66
Grade 8	♩	=	132	♩.	=	76

Trombone

major and minor scales, chromatic scales, whole-tone scales, dominant and diminished sevenths				*major and minor arpeggios*		
Grade 1	♩	=	44	♪	=	66
Grade 2	♩	=	48	♪	=	72
Grade 3	♩	=	56	♪	=	84
Grade 4	♩	=	63	♪	=	92
Grade 5	♩	=	72	♪	=	104
Grade 6	♩	=	96	♩.	=	46
Grade 7	♩	=	108	♩.	=	56
Grade 8	♩	=	120	♩.	=	60

Major Scales

1 C MAJOR 1 Octave

1 Valved instruments: make sure that 3 goes down simultaneously with 1 on D. Listen carefully to the intonation on D, using the 3rd valve slide or 4th valve (where available) to compensate. Do not let the tone thin out as you ascend.
Trombone: in order to avoid sharpness, make sure that you extend the slide fully to 6th position for D.

2 C MAJOR A Twelfth

3 C MAJOR 2 Octaves

3 Trumpet/B♭ Cornet/Flugelhorn/Tenor Horn: top C is sometimes a little flat, especially on older instruments; try 1 instead of the open fingering. Do not just press harder on the mouthpiece for the highest notes; keep the corners of the embouchure still.

4 D♭ MAJOR A Twelfth

4 Trombone: calculate the slide positions carefully at the top of this scale in order to avoid intonation problems.

5 D MAJOR 1 Octave

5 All instruments: keep the tone as full as possible as you ascend.
Valved instruments: listen carefully to the intonation of both Ds, compensating with either the 3rd valve slide or the 4th valve where available.
Trombone: tune F♯ carefully.

6 D MAJOR A Twelfth

6 Valved instruments: take care to keep the highest notes of this scale (especially A³) really centred.

7 E♭ MAJOR 1 Octave

7 Valved instruments: fingering 2+3 to 1 and back (E♭ to F) needs careful co-ordination.
Trombone: tune low E♭ and A♭ carefully.

8 E♭ MAJOR A Twelfth

3

9 E MAJOR 1 Octave

9 Valved instruments: co-ordinate the fingering from G♯ to A carefully (2+3 to 1+2).
Trumpet/Cornets/Flugelhorn: listen carefully to the intonation on low and high E which may be sharp and flat respectively. Alternative fingerings are worth investigating here.

10 E MAJOR A Twelfth

Grade 4

11 F MAJOR 1 Octave

11 Baritone/Euphonium: listen carefully to top F which tends to be sharp. Use 1+4 for top F if the 4th valve is available.
Trombone: do not let the tone thin out as you ascend.

12 F MAJOR A Twelfth

12 Valved instruments: listen carefully to the intonation of top C, which may be flat. Try 1 instead of the open fingering. Do not just press harder on the mouthpiece for the highest notes; keep the corners of the embouchure still.
Trombone: remember to maintain a firm diaphragm support throughout, especially at the top over the turn--around. Do not relax the embouchure too soon.

13 F♯ MAJOR 2 Octaves

13 All instruments: take care with the production of the lowest notes in this scale; keep the tone as uniform as possible.
Tenor Horn/Euphonium/Tuba: use 2+4 for F♯¹ if the 4th valve is available.

14 G MAJOR 2 Octaves

14 Valved instruments: special care must be taken to preserve uniformity of tone and intonation across the range.
Tenor Horn/Euphonium/Tuba: use the 4th valve where available for G¹.
Baritone/Euphonium: top F♯ and G will tend to be sharp; use 2+4 and 4 for these notes where the 4th valve is available.

Grade 4

15 A♭ MAJOR A Twelfth

15 Valved instruments: low D♭ needs careful tuning; compensate with either the 3rd valve slide or the 4th valve where available.

16 A♭ MAJOR 2 Octaves

16 Valved instruments: low D♭ needs careful tuning; compensate with either the 3rd valve slide or the 4th valve where available. Special care must be taken to preserve uniformity of tone and intonation across the range.
Trombone: top A♭ (A♭³) tends to be flat; tune it carefully.

3 **17 A MAJOR** A Twelfth

17 Valved instruments: listen carefully to the intonation of C#^{1} and D^1, compensating with the 3rd valve slide or the 4th valve where available.
Trombone: make sure that you extend the slide fully to 7th position for C#^{1}; use the 'F' valve alternative (V^2), where available.

18 A MAJOR 2 Octaves

18 Baritone/Euphonium/Tuba: take care to centre both pitch and tone of the top three notes of this scale.
Trombone: top A tends to be flat; tune it carefully.

19 B♭ MAJOR 1 Octave

19 Valved instruments: listen carefully to the intonation on D^1, compensating with the 3rd valve slide or 4th valve, where available.
Trombone: listen carefully to the tuning of E♭, both ascending and descending.

Grade 4
20 B♭ MAJOR A Twelfth

20 Baritone/Euphonium: listen carefully to top F, which tends to be sharp. Use 1+4 for top F if the 4th valve is available.

21 B♭ MAJOR 2 Octaves

21 E♭ Soprano Cornet: remember to maintain a firm diaphragm support over the turn-around at the top of this scale.
Baritone/Euphonium: listen carefully to top F and G, which tend to be sharp. Use 1+4 and 4 respectively for these notes, where the 4th valve is available.
Trombone: top B♭ will need extra diaphragm support to maintain the tonal uniformity of this scale.

22 B MAJOR A Twelfth

22 E♭ Soprano Cornet: listen carefully to the intonation in the lower notes of this scale.
Trombone: make sure that you extend the slide fully to 7th position for low C#, tuning the following D# really carefully. Where available, use the 'F' valve alternative (V^2), listening carefully to the intonation.

23 B MAJOR 2 Octaves

23 Tenor Horn/Baritone/Euphonium: listen carefully to top B, which tends to be flat.
Trombone: make sure that you extend the slide fully to 7th position for low C#, tuning the following D# really carefully. Where available, use the 'F' valve alternative (V^2), listening carefully to the intonation.

Minor Scales

24 C MINOR melodic
1 Octave

24 and **25 Valved instruments:** fingering 1+3 to 2+3 (D to E♭) will need careful co-ordination.

25 C MINOR harmonic
1 Octave

26 C MINOR melodic
A Twelfth

27 C MINOR harmonic
A Twelfth

28 C MINOR melodic
2 Octaves

29 C MINOR harmonic
2 Octaves

30 C♯ MINOR melodic
A Twelfth

31 C♯ MINOR harmonic
A Twelfth

32 D MINOR melodic
1 Octave

32 and **33** **All instruments**: keep the tone as full as possible as you ascend.
Valved instruments: listen carefully to the intonation of both Ds, compensating with either the 3rd valve slide or the 4th valve where available.

33 D MINOR harmonic
1 Octave

34 D MINOR melodic
A Twelfth

34 and **35** **Trombone**: top A tends to be flat; tune it carefully.

35 D MINOR harmonic
A Twelfth

36 E♭ MINOR melodic
A Twelfth

36 and **37** **Trombone**: for top A♭ and B♭, calculate the 3rd position difference very carefully.

37 E♭ MINOR harmonic
A Twelfth

38 E MINOR melodic
1 Octave

39 E MINOR harmonic
1 Octave

39 **Trombone**: the interval C to D♯ needs careful pitching.

40 E MINOR melodic
A Twelfth

46 and **47 Trombone**: listen carefully to the intonation of top E♯.

50 G MINOR melodic
2 Octaves

50 and 51 **Valved instruments**: special care must be taken to preserve uniformity of tone and intonation across the range.
Tenor Horn/Euphonium/Tuba: use the 4th valve where available for G^1.
Baritone/Euphonium: top F, F# and G will tend to be sharp; use 1+4, 2+4 and 4 for these notes where the 4th valve is available.

51 G MINOR harmonic
2 Octaves

52 G# MINOR melodic
2 Octaves

53 G# MINOR harmonic
2 Octaves

54 A MINOR melodic
1 Octave

54 and 55 **All instruments**: take care with the production of the lowest notes of these scales. Keep the tone as uniform and as focused as possible.

55 A MINOR harmonic
1 Octave

55 **Valved instruments**: fingering 1 to 2+3 and back (F to G#) needs careful co-ordination.

56 A MINOR melodic
A Twelfth

Grade 4

57 A MINOR harmonic
A Twelfth

58 A MINOR melodic
2 Octaves

59 A MINOR harmonic
2 Octaves

60 Bb MINOR melodic
A Twelfth

60 and **61 Eb Soprano Cornet**: listen carefully to the intonation in the lower notes of these scales.

61 Bb MINOR harmonic
A Twelfth

62 Bb MINOR melodic
2 Octaves

62 and **63 Eb Soprano Cornet**: remember to maintain a firm diaphragm support over the turn-around at the top of these scales.

63 Bb MINOR harmonic
2 Octaves

64 B MINOR melodic
A Twelfth

64 and **65 Baritone/Euphonium**: top F# will tend to be sharp; use 2+4 where the 4th valve is available.

Grade 4

65 B MINOR harmonic
A Twelfth

66 B MINOR melodic
2 Octaves

67 B MINOR harmonic
2 Octaves

Chromatic Scales

NOTE: the breath must be gauged very carefully for 2-octave chromatic scales.
Tenor Horn/Euphonium/Tuba: where available, the use of the 4th valve is essential in the chromatic scale, both to aid intonation and develop fluency in its use.
Trombone: in all chromatic scales, take special care to keep the slide movement quick and precise.

68 on C 1 Octave

68 Valved instruments: listen carefully to the intonation of $C\sharp^1$ and D^1, compensating wih the 3rd valve slide or 4th valve, where available.

69 on C A Twelfth

70 on C 2 Octaves

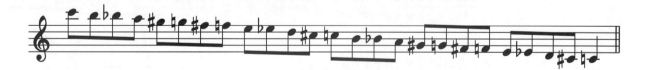

71 on D 1 Octave

71 Trombone: the slide movement between G and G♯ needs careful negotiation.

72 on F 1 Octave

73 on F# 2 Octaves

73–76 **All instruments**: aim to preserve uniformity of sound throughout the range, especially when descending.

74 on G 2 Octaves

74 **Trombone**: if using the 'F' valve, co-ordinate slide and LH thumb movement really carefully.

75 on A♭ 2 Octaves

76 on A 2 Octaves

grade 4

77 on B♭ A Twelfth

77 **Baritone/Euphonium**: top F will tend to be sharp; use 1+4 for this note where the 4th valve is available.

78 on B♭ 2 Octaves

78 Trombone: top B♭ will need extra support to maintain the tonal uniformity of this scale.

79 on B 2 Octaves

Whole-Tone Scales

80 on A 2 Octaves

80 and **81 E♭ Soprano Cornet:** fingering co-ordination and intonation need special care in the lower part of the range.

81 on B♭ 2 Octaves

82 on B 2 Octaves

83 on C 2 Octaves

Major Arpeggios

84 C MAJOR 1 Octave

84 All instruments: take special care when negotiating G to C and back, especially when slurred, or *legato*-tongued.

85 C MAJOR A Twelfth

86 C MAJOR 2 Octaves

86 Trombone: calculate the interval between top G and C really carefully (top C often emerges as top B♭).

87 D♭ MAJOR A Twelfth

87 Valved instruments: on low D♭, use the 3rd valve slide or the 4th valve to compensate where available.
Trombone: for top F and A♭, calculate the 3rd position difference very carefully.

88 D MAJOR 1 Octave

88 Valved instruments: finger co-ordination needs care throughout, especially when slurred; using the 4th valve on the euphonium and tuba where available will eradicate this problem and improve intonation.
Trumpet/Cornets/Flugelhorn: listen carefully to the intonation of both Ds.

89 D MAJOR A Twelfth

89 All instruments: keep a really centred sound on top A.

90 E♭ MAJOR 1 Octave

90 Valved instruments: use 2+3 for top E♭ if 2 is flat; listen carefully.

91 E♭ MAJOR A Twelfth

92 E MAJOR 1 Octave

92 Valved instruments: use 1+2 for top E if the open fingering is flat; listen carefully.

93 E MAJOR A Twelfth

Grade 4
94 F MAJOR 1 Octave

94 Trombone: support the sound carefully from C to F and back, especially when *legato*-tonguing.

95 F MAJOR A Twelfth

95 Trumpet/Cornets/Flugelhorn/Tenor Horn: listen carefully to the intonation of top C, which may be flat. Try 1 instead of the open fingering.

96 F♯ MAJOR 2 Octaves

96 and **97 All instruments:** take care to preserve uniformity of sound throughout the range, especially when descending.

97 G MAJOR 2 Octaves

Grade 4
98 A♭ MAJOR A Twelfth

99 A♭ MAJOR 2 Octaves

100 A MAJOR A Twelfth

100 and **101 Valved instruments**: listen carefully to the intonation on C♯^{1} and E^2.

101 A MAJOR 2 Octaves

102 B♭ MAJOR 1 Octave

102 Valved instruments: listen carefully to the intonation
on D, compensating with the 3rd valve slide or 4th valve
where available.

grade 4

103 B♭ MAJOR A Twelfth

103 and **104 Valved instruments**: as most of the notes in these arpeggios are
played with the 1st valve, lip flexibility must be carefully calculated, especially when
slurred.

104 B♭ MAJOR 2 Octaves

104 E♭ Soprano Cornet: remember to maintain a firm diaphragm support over
the turn-around at the top of this arpeggio.

105 B MAJOR A Twelfth

106 B MAJOR 2 Octaves

Minor Arpeggios

107 C MINOR 1 Octave

108 C MINOR A Twelfth

109 C MINOR 2 Octaves

109 Trombone: calculate the interval between top G and C really carefully (top C often emerges as top B♭).

110 C# MINOR A Twelfth

110 Valved instruments: listen carefully to the intonation on low C♯, compensating with the 3rd valve slide or 4th valve where available.

111 D MINOR 1 Octave

111 Valved instruments: listen carefully to the intonation on low D, compensating with the 3rd valve slide or 4th valve where available.

112 D MINOR A Twelfth

113 E♭ MINOR A Twelfth

114 E MINOR 1 Octave

114 Trumpet/Cornets/Flugelhorn: listen carefully to the intonation on low and high E which may be sharp and flat respectively. Alternative fingerings are worth investigating here.
Trombone: take special care to support the sound from B to E and back, especially when *legato*-tonguing.

115 E MINOR A Twelfth

Grade 4

116 F MINOR 1 Octave

117 F MINOR A Twelfth

118 F# MINOR 1 Octave

119 F# MINOR 2 Octaves

120 G MINOR 2 Octaves

120 **All instruments**: take care to preseve uniformity of sound throughout the range, especially when descending.

121 G# MINOR 2 Octaves

122 A MINOR 1 Octave

122 **Valved instruments**: keep the tone on low A as steady as possible. Take special care when negotiating E to A and back, especially when slurred.

Grade 4

123 A MINOR A Twelfth

123 and 124 **Valved instruments**: lip flexibility needs care here, especially when slurred.

124 A MINOR 2 Octaves

125 Bb MINOR A Twelfth

125 Eb Soprano Cornet: listen carefully to the intonation in the lower notes of this arpeggio.

126 Bb MINOR 2 Octaves

126 Valved instruments: take care when negotiating top F to top Bb and back, especially when slurred.
Eb Soprano Cornet: remember to maintain a firm diaphragm support over the turn-around at the top of this arpeggio. Listen carefully to the intonation of the lower notes.

grade 4

127 B MINOR A Twelfth

128 B MINOR 2 Octaves

Dominant Sevenths

129–135 Trumpet/Bb Cornet/Flugelhorn: practising the notes within brackets with the given fingering, thereby using the harmonic series, makes a useful exercise in lip flexibility.

129 in C 2 Octaves

130 in Db 2 Octaves

131 in D 2 Octaves

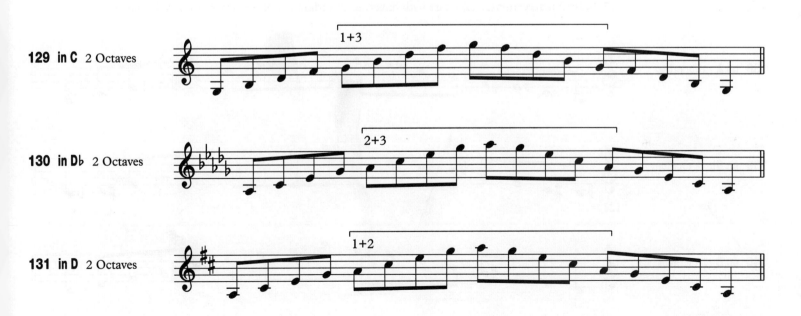

132 in E♭ 2 Octaves

133 in E 2 Octaves

134 in F 2 Octaves

135 in B 2 Octaves

Diminished Sevenths

136 on G 2 Octaves

137 on A♭ 2 Octaves

137 Valved instruments: take care with fingering co-ordination of the lower notes in this arpeggio.

138 on A 2 Octaves

139 on B♭ 2 Octaves

140 on B 2 Octaves

Music and text origination by
Barnes Music Engraving Ltd, East Sussex
Printed by Caligraving Ltd, Thetford, Norfolk